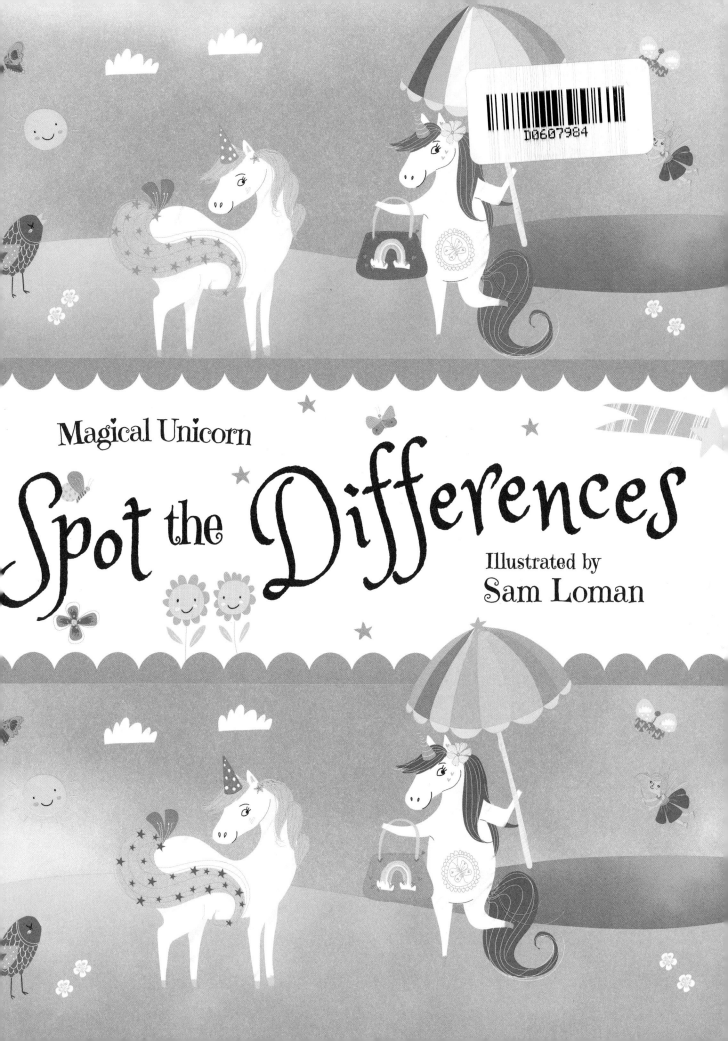

Magical Unicorn

Spot the Differences

Illustrated by
Sam Loman

Bibliographical Note

This Dover edition, first published in 2019, is a slightly altered
republication of the work illustrated by Sam Loman and written
by Anna Brett, which was originally published by Arcturus Publishing
Limited, London, in 2018.

International Standard Book Number

ISBN-13: 978-0-486-83229-6
ISBN-10: 0-486-83229-5

Manufactured in the United States by LSC Communications
83229504   2020
www.doverpublications.com

Best Friends Forever

These two unicorns are best friends! They try to always look the same, but can you find and circle six differences between them?

Rainbow Magic

Unicorns can change their hair to match the colors in a rainbow!

Find and circle ten differences in the eye-catching scene below.

Cupcake Count

The unicorns are setting the table for cake, but one of their yummy treats looks a bit different. Circle the one that is different.

Beautiful Butterflies

These butterflies have just hatched and are spreading their wings for the first time. Can you find and circle six differences in the bottom scene?

KITTEN KISSES

Willow has come to visit her cat friend, Cloudy, and her new kittens!

They are having so much fun, climbing over everything in sight.
Can you find and circle ten differences in the image below?

Reindeer Replacements

Santa's reindeer are not feeling well! Luckily he's called on his unicorn friends to help pull the magic sleigh tonight.

While Santa delivers his gifts, see if you can find and circle ten differences in the scene below.

Little Ones

All the mothers have brought their babies along to the meadow to play together. Can you circle six differences in the bottom picture?

Fancy Dress

These unicorns are all dressing up as fairies for the costume party!
Which unicorn looks different from the others?

SPARKLING SEA

The unicorns are having a boat party!

Can you find and circle ten things that have changed in the picture below?

Dream Wings

Unicorns love to dream that they can fly high
in the sky, in and out of the clouds.

Can you find and circle ten
differences in the picture below?

Quickstep

Twinkletoes is trying to copy Stardust's dance moves, but she has three of the steps wrong. Can you identify which three steps she needs to work on?

Stardust

1 2 3 4 5

Twinkletoes

1 2 3 4 5

Winter Wonderland

It's snowing! Time to build some snow-unicorns, but watch out for the snowball fight! Find and circle six differences in the bottom scene.

Falling Leaves

Moondust is dancing in the leaves at dusk.

Can you find and circle ten differences in the scene below?

Splish Splash

The unicorns are playing with the mermaids
in the rock pool today.

Find ten differences between the two watery scenes and
circle them in the picture below.

BEACH BAG

It's time to hit the beach! Which unicorn's bag looks slightly different from the rest?

Love Is in the Air

Cupid is spreading love today, and everyone is thinking of their loved ones! Can you find and circle six differences in the bottom scene?

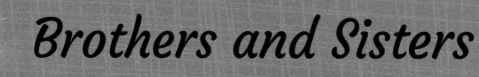

Brothers and Sisters

These puppy pets are all from the same litter!

Find and circle ten differences in the scene on this page.

Sleepover Snuggles

These three unicorns are having a sleepover tonight. They look so comfy with their soft blankets, puffy cushions, and sweet treats.

Look at the two pictures and see if you can circle all
ten differences in the dreamy scene below.

TIME TO SHINE

Glitter has just completed a perfect round at the competition! Sunray's round was not so successful. Can you circle the five mistakes she made?

Prize Giving

It's time for the Rainbow Awards! There are six differences between the two ceremonies—find and circle them in the bottom picture.

Salon Style

It's busy in the Picture Perfect Salon today
because Snowflake wants her mane and tail decorated.

Look at the two scenes, and then see if you can
circle all ten differences in the picture below.

33

Fairy Ring

It's finally summer, and the fairies are starting their party!

On the picture below, find and circle the ten differences between the two gatherings.

CLOUD SPOTTING

These unicorns are looking up at the clouds in the sky.
When the wind blows, the shapes change. See if you can find
six changes in the bottom picture.

Flower Arranging

These two bouquets of flowers are being delivered to the palace, but they should match. Can you circle the four flowers that are arranged differently in the bouquet on the right?

Princess Palace

These unicorns can't wait to visit the pink palace today.

Can you find ten differences in the two royal scenes?
Circle them in the image below.

Whiz, Pop, Bang!

The unicorns are enjoying watching fireworks in the sky.

The magical display changes quickly, though. Can you spot the ten differences in the picture below?

LUCKY CAKES

These cupcakes have been decorated with lucky unicorn shoes. Three of the decorations are upside down—can you find and circle them?

Flower Crown

Sunshine has made a flower crown for Blossom.
See if you can find and circle six things that have changed
in the bottom picture.

Round and Round

Unicorns love riding on rollercoasters . . . as long as the loop-the-loop
doesn't make them too dizzy!

Can you find and circle ten differences
in the speedy ride below?

Birthday Party

It's Starshine's birthday, and her unicorn friends have arranged a surprise party for her!

Can you see ten changes that have
taken place during the party?
Circle them in the picture below.

OPEN WATER

These mermaids are going on a trip away from their home on the reef.
Can you find and circle six changes in the scene on the bottom?

Puppy Pairs

This unicorn is babysitting seven cute puppies. Three pairs are twins—can you match them up? Which puppy does not have a twin?

Shopping Trip

It's time to hit the shops with your best unicorn friends!

Can you find and circle ten differences in the super-fun shopping scene below?

End of the Rainbow

These unicorns have found the magical end of the rainbow!

The rainbow is beautiful, but can you circle ten things
that have changed in the image below?

Fairy Dust

The Fairy Godmother is sprinkling magic on Bluebell to help her get ready for a special party. Can you circle the change that took place after each wave of the Fairy Godmother's wand?

Royal Jewels

The princess is showing her unicorn friend all her beautiful jewels.
Can you find six differences between the two jewelry boxes?
Circle the changes in the jewelry box on the right.

Ice Skating

Unicorns love to skate—slipping and sliding is so much fun!

Not everyone is always steady on their hooves.
Can you circle ten differences in the picture below?

Ballet School

Point those hooves, and twirl that tail! Ballet class is in full swing.

Find and circle ten differences
in the image below.

KITTEN TANGLE

These cute kitties are playing with their unicorn friend.
Can you find and circle six changes in the scene at the bottom?

Perfect Patterns

These unicorns have had their hooves and bodies painted! They all have matching designs, except for one. Who looks different?

Christmas Carols

Fa la la, it's time for the annual holiday concert!

There are ten differences between these two festive scenes.
Circle the changes in the image below.

Sweet Dreams

What do unicorns dream about at night?
Look at the picture to find out.

Find and circle ten differences in the picture below.

BUTTERFLIES AND BEES

It's springtime, and the bees and butterflies are playing
in the beautiful blooms. Every creature has a twin, except for one.
Can you find and circle it?

Yummy Ice Creams

It's hot today! All the unicorns are enjoying ice creams to help them
to cool down. Find the six differences between the two scenes.
Circle them in the bottom picture.

Carnival Fun

There's so much to do at the fair!

Can you find and circle ten changes below
that make the picture different?

Coral Reef

Take a deep breath and dive underwater to see all the
amazing marine life on the reef.

What ten things have changed as the unicorns
swim along in the scene below? Circle them.

SKI SLOPE

The unicorns slip and slide down the slope on skis. Can you spot and circle six differences in the snowy scene on the bottom?

Uni-yoga

Unicorns love a good stretch! Find and circle one of the members of the yoga class who has a different pose.

Gingerbread House

Deep in the forest, there's a secret gingerbread house.

It looks as if unicorns may have sampled
some of the sweet decorations in the picture below.
Can you circle ten differences?

Magical Music

These unicorn friends have formed a band, The Rainbow Rockers,
and they hope to be famous one day!

Can you spot ten differences between the two jam sessions and circle them below?

Fruit Picking

These berries are ripe for the picking. Can you find six differences between the two rows of bushes? Circle the changes in the bottom row.

Beautiful Blankets

There is a blanket for each unicorn. Circle the two blankets that are different in the bottom picture.

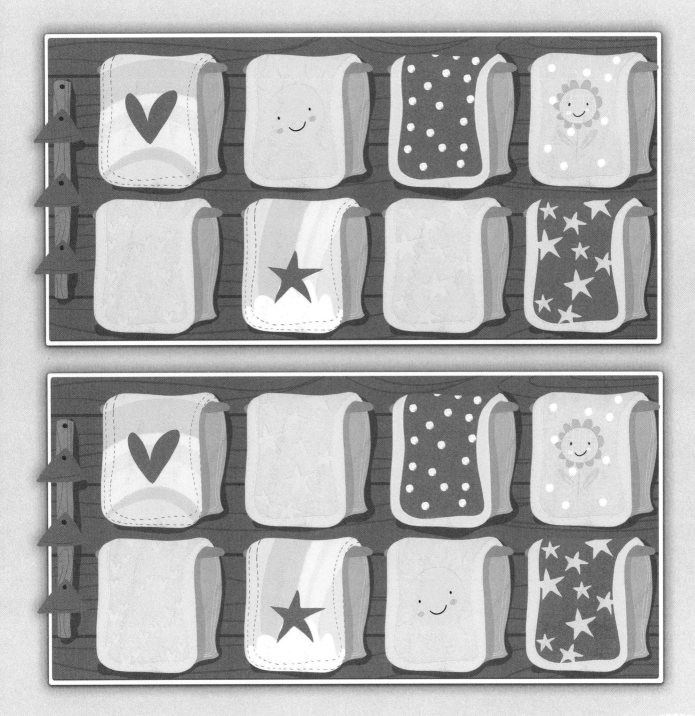

Mermaid Kingdom

King Poseidon is hosting a feast for all the merpeople!

Find and circle ten differences in the underwater scene below.

Outer Space

Moonbeam is the first unicorn in space!

What wonders can she see on her space mission?
Find and circle ten differences in the starry scene below.

PICNIC IN THE PARK

Dragonfly and Roseleaf are enjoying a yummy picnic.
Can you circle six differences in the bottom scene?

84

Pixie Parade

It's time for the annual pixie parade!
Can you find and circle the pixie that looks a bit different?

Royal Wedding

Today is the day the fairy prince
marries his fairy princess!

Everyone is so happy, and there's so much going on in the palace.
Can you spot and circle ten differences in the picture below?

Sunset Sky

These unicorns are watching the sun set over the ocean.
Can you find and circle six differences in the bottom scene?

Answers

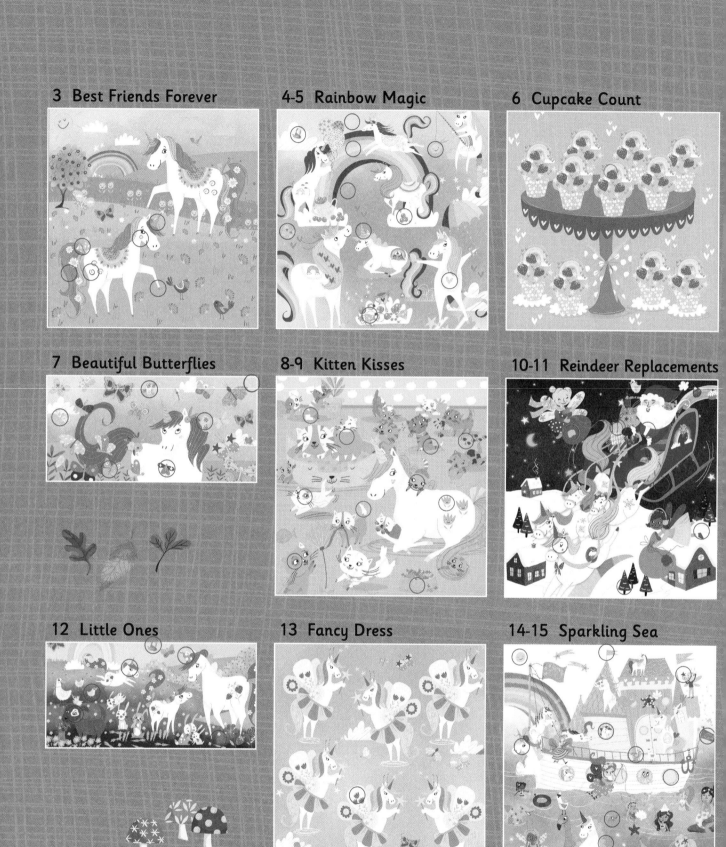

3 Best Friends Forever

4-5 Rainbow Magic

6 Cupcake Count

7 Beautiful Butterflies

8-9 Kitten Kisses

10-11 Reindeer Replacements

12 Little Ones

13 Fancy Dress

14-15 Sparkling Sea

16-17 Dream Wings

18 Quickstep

19 Winter Wonderland

20-21 Falling Leaves

22-23 Splish Splash

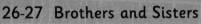

24 Beach Bag

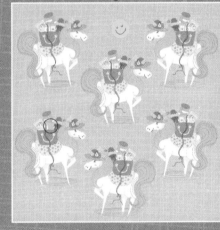

25 Love Is in the Air

26-27 Brothers and Sisters

28-29 Sleepover Snuggles

30 Time to Shine

31 Prize Giving

32-33 Salon Style

34-35 Fairy Ring

36 Cloud Spotting

37 Flower Arranging

38-39 Princess Palace

40-41 Whiz, Pop, Bang!

42 Lucky Cakes

43 Flower Crown

44-45 Round and Round

46-47 Birthday Party

48 Open Water

49 Puppy Pairs

50-51 Shopping Trip

52-53 End of the Rainbow

54 Fairy Dust

55 Royal Jewels

56-57 Ice Skating

58-59 Ballet School

60 Kitten Tangle

61 Perfect Patterns

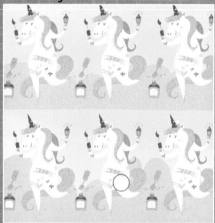

62-63 Christmas Carols

64-65 Sweet Dreams

66 Butterflies and Bees

67 Yummy Ice Creams

68-69 Carnival Fun

70-71 Coral Reef

72 Ski Slope

73 Uni-yoga

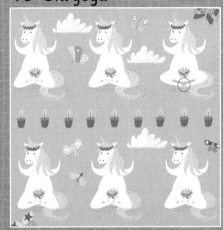

74-75 Gingerbread House

76-77 Magical Music

78 Fruit Picking

79 Beautiful Blankets

80-81 Mermaid Kingdom

82-83 Outer Space

84 Picnic in the Park

85 Pixie Parade

86-87 Royal Wedding

88 Sunset Sky